THE HARE WITH GREEN EYES AND OTHER STORIES

By Paula Page

For my mum, who always wondered where I got it from, and Ian, who let me run with it no matter what.

FOREWORD

Discovering I had a tale or two to tell, relatively late in life, has been a surprise and an absolute joy to me, opening doors to places I barely knew existed…like Widnes!

I'm a proud member of the Adult Creative Writing Group at The Studio, Widnes. I can say with confidence that it would be hard to find a more welcoming and supportive collection of people, lead with unerring enthusiasm by our tutor Wayne Cookson, encouraging us every step of the way.

The short stories and poems in this book have been produced during the last two years which, for many reasons, have in turn been the strangest and most wonderful of my life so far. Like my mum, I have no idea where they came from. I'm just glad they did.

The author retains copyright of all of her work contained within this collection © 2020

Published by Feeedback Publishing.

The Creative Writing Sessions, which helped to produce these stories, were held at The Studio, Lacey Street, Widnes WA8 7SQ during 2019/20. These sessions were part of the "All Together Now" Reaching Communities project made possible thanks to funding to LOOSE by The National Lottery Community Fund.

LOOSE is a registered Charity 1153066
Non-profit company LBG 6566823

Contact: info@thestudiowidnes.org.uk
www.thestudiowidnes.org.uk

Stories

Wild Woodbines
The Hare With Green Eyes
The House With Three Floors
A Mermaid In The River Alt
The Musings of An Ancient Oak
Always Read the Small Print
Cut and Shut
The Last Unicorn
The Dragon of Dam Wood

Poetry

The Illustrated Man
Thank you
What if

Credits

The Studio Widnes
Louise Nulty
Photography: Tom Barton
All illustrations by the author
Edited by Wayne Cookson

NEMs ENTERPRISES
THE NORTH'S No 1 COMBO
THE
BEATLES
PARLAPHONE RECORDING ARTISTS
AT THE
QUEEN'S HALL
WIDNES
FOR THREE MONDAY NIGHTS
SEPTEMBER 3RD 10TH & 17TH
7·30 TO 11 PM
A BOB WOOLER production - OF COURSE!
SENSATIONAL GROUPS - INCLUDING
BILLY KRAMER with the Coasters
RORY STORM and the Hurricanes
SONNY KAYE and the Reds
PRICE 3/6
TICKETS AVAILABLE FROM: RUSHWORTH'S, NEMS, STROTHERS, TOP HAT RECORD BAR, LEWIS'S, CRANES & THE QUEEN'S HALL

WILD WOODBINES

Funny how the strangest things can spark off a memory.

Woodbines. Just the word made her smile. *Who even knows what a Woodbine is these days?* You definitely had to be of a certain age. Thing was, her nose was being enveloped by the slightly acrid, oddly comforting aroma of Woodbines right now and she knew this wasn't right... *For one thing they stopped selling them donkeys years ago and for another I'm indoors. You can't smoke inside public places, not even in Widnes.*

I'll put you out of your misery. A Woodbine was a brand of cigarette, tiny and nasty like stunted mistakes. You certainly wouldn't catch Audrey Hepburn with one of those dangling out of the end of her elegant cigarette holder.

These malformed excuses for tobacco made Karen think of her grandmother and for some reason that made her smile. Not like a Cheshire Cat, no, more like puzzled and bemused. Why wouldn't she smile? She was remembering her Nan after all. Well, her Nan wasn't the cuddly type. She subscribed to the

Joan Crawford school of parenting. In fact she was decidedly cold and the only love she seemed to have was for those vile cigarettes. She must have wheezed and coughed her way through thousands of them before they shuffled her off this mortal coil…One thing Karen did remember was the packet, tiny like the toy cigarettes children were encouraged to buy in the 1970's, the artwork almost as pretty and ornate as a William Morris print. All the more perverse when you consider that they ultimately killed you.

So why could she smell them now?

Karen was looking around the Queen's Hall in Widnes. She was checking it out as a possible venue for the theatre company she volunteered with. So far she could go either way. The place was dark and a bit dingy, with an overwhelming air of being well past its sell by date. It had a lack of warmth; actually, it was freezing. Karen was one of these women who had to deal with being perpetually hot and bothered, but she hadn't even thought about taking her coat off, it was that cold. However, the people running the place were friendly and best of all it was cheap to hire…always a plus point! It definitely had something about it, something she couldn't put her finger on but it was enough to make her curious. And, of course, there was that smell…

The girl showing her around seemed nice enough. Karen didn't want to offend her by saying the place had a funny smell, so she kept that observation to herself. There was another reason for this though.

She wasn't sure that what she could smell was real. Not that she believed it was anything supernatural, far from it: she was very much a sceptic. Her real fear was that it was something quite different. An olfactory hallucination. Smelling something that wasn't real. You see, Karen had Parkinson's disease and the thing that terrified her more than anything was the thought that she was losing her mind, seeing, hearing or even smelling things that simply did not exist.

She quickly gave herself a good talking to. She did this a lot, inside her head of course; this was where she was always most eloquent and articulate. Then she got on with the task in hand.

"This stage is amazing; I think it could be perfect for what we want to do. It looks like it's been here forever! When was the place built?" she asked the girl.

"Actually, it was opened in 1864. We've had all kinds here: from the Beatles in 1962 right through to clubbers not so long ago."

Karen was taken aback by this. Here she was contemplating using a venue that had been used by The Beatles! She was from Liverpool, but she'd never even been in The Cavern. Not that The Cavern was the real deal, it was a fake set up for the tourists. This place, however, was.

Then she felt it, that sickening stab of pain in her stomach that was the signal a nausea attack was on its way. Another symptom of Parkinson's...the gift that keeps on giving.

She'd been living with this uninvited guest for nearly ten years, treating it with the contempt it deserved. It was a thief. Actually, it was more like a compulsive shoplifter. Every day it would raise its ugly head, regular as clockwork, as her myriad of drugs wore off and it would take part of Karen away without her permission. As time went on it was clear to Karen that the battle to retain her healthy self was getting harder and harder. She didn't want, and wasn't ready, to disappear.

She was always upfront about her illness, she never hid it. Sometimes people were kind and said things like, "Really? You have that? Well, you wouldn't know, you look fine!" She'd smile inwardly thinking, *ok then do you want to swap?* But she'd never say that out loud. Other times people thought her tremor was a sign of nerves, or that her occasional static expression meant she was worried. She'd put them right about that and usually crack a joke about how she was never going to realise her ambition to be a spy or a poker player, but she probably could get a minor part in "River Dance."

For God's sake...She hadn't had a nausea attack for ages, months even. Of all the times to get one! It would pass, but she needed ten or fifteen minutes to get over it.

She made her excuses and went to the ladies. She put the seat down on the loo and felt the cold molestation of sweat travelling up her body. This was going to be a bad one. She didn't close her eyes, she didn't want to lose control, but suddenly everything went black.

There was that smell again, but stronger. Woodies and something else. God, it was sweat! It felt warm too, like the place was full; she could hear music, but it was muffled and distorted, like a radio that was only half tuned in to the station.

No that couldn't be right, it was just me and that girl a minute ago...

Then again, she wasn't on the toilet now either; she was backstage. Just in front of her, quite beautifully lit, was a young skinny man dressed all in black. He was smoking a Woodbine.

"Who are you?" she asked.

"Well, I'm not John, obviously," the man replied.
"John who?"

He started laughing when she said that. Not like it was funny, but in a bitter, fed up sort of way. He exhaled slowly and deliberately. Karen watched, transfixed as the tendrils of smoke almost seemed to dance in time, through his slicked back hair to the white noise in the background before travelling skyward.

"Everyone wants to see John; when they get me I can sense the profound disappointment immediately. They don't have to say a word. It's there in their eyes."

He had a flat Scouse accent, discordant, practically monotone, and Karen did not have a clue what he was going on about. *This is definitely the meds, or maybe this is it and I'm on my way to dementia. What the hell, I'll go along with it, no point in fighting.*

"John who?" she repeated.

He turned around then and, for the first time, she saw his face in sharp focus. No more silhouette, the smoke had been chased away.

"Lennon of course. John Lennon. They all want him. Nobody is arsed about George."

She couldn't help it, maybe it was nerves, but she burst out laughing! Then she looked at him. These meds were good! This young man was the absolute spit of George Harrison.

Sod it! If I'm hallucinating, at least it's a good one and I might as well embrace it.

Karen was a funny girl. Your first impression of her would probably be that she was reserved, quiet to the point of being painfully shy. However, on occasion, when the mood took her, she could be cocky and smart, some might even say a bit of a smart arse. Today was one of those days. After all, it wasn't every day you got to talk to a deceased Beatle.

"Actually, I think you are making quite an assumption there."

This obviously disarmed the figure in black because, for a split second, he looked genuinely surprised. He quickly recovered himself and resumed his sardonic world weary persona.

"Go on, enlighten me. What do you mean by that?"

"Well...not everyone thought John was the best or most talented one you know. In fact I thought his was a bit of a tool to be honest. I can't be doing with "Imagine." It's one of the most depressing songs I've ever heard. Give me "Here comes the Sun" or "My Sweet Lord" any day of the week. As for "Something," well that moves me to tears... in a good way of course." She felt a bit braver now. "Can I ask you a question? Are you a ghost or what? You were a lot older than this when you...you know...died."

He rolled his eyes. "What do you think I am? A figment of your imagination? Put yourself in my shoes. I was 58 when I went and to be honest I wasn't looking my best, who is? If you've got to come back, why not look like you did when you were in your prime?"

Karen had never really thought about it before but it did make a lot of sense. Unbelievably, she'd just said that she thought John Lennon was a bit of a tool to someone who actually knew him! But she knew no fear now and she spoke her mind.

"OK then George, shall we put this into perspective? You were a Beatle for God's sake! How many people can say that? A hero to generations of people all over the world; be content. It could be a lot worse… you could have been Ringo!"

He laughed and his eyes seemed to smile as he looked at her.

"Say what you think why don't you? I suppose you're right, but we all have our insecurities, even one of The Beatles, believe it or not. Anyway, thanks love. I want to listen to these now, they're alright…might even make something of themselves."

He turned away from her, casually took another Woodbine from its resting place above his ear, lit it and carried on watching the band on stage.

The white noise suddenly became deafening and she started to feel the cold sweat making an unwelcome return. The darkness and the stage gave way to the brightly lit toilet cubicle. Karen looked at her watch; it was only a matter of minutes since she had first rushed in there! Then it hit her. She couldn't smell Woodbines any more.

Well that was bizarre. I suppose I'll have to let the Parkinson's nurse know my meds need upping...again.

After saying her goodbyes, she left the hall and started the long journey back to Liverpool on the bus. To pass the time, she began to rifle through her seemingly bottomless bag to see if she had the nurse's phone number, *no point in putting off the inevitable.* It was then that she noticed the small, open packet of Wild Woodbine cigarettes looking back at her.

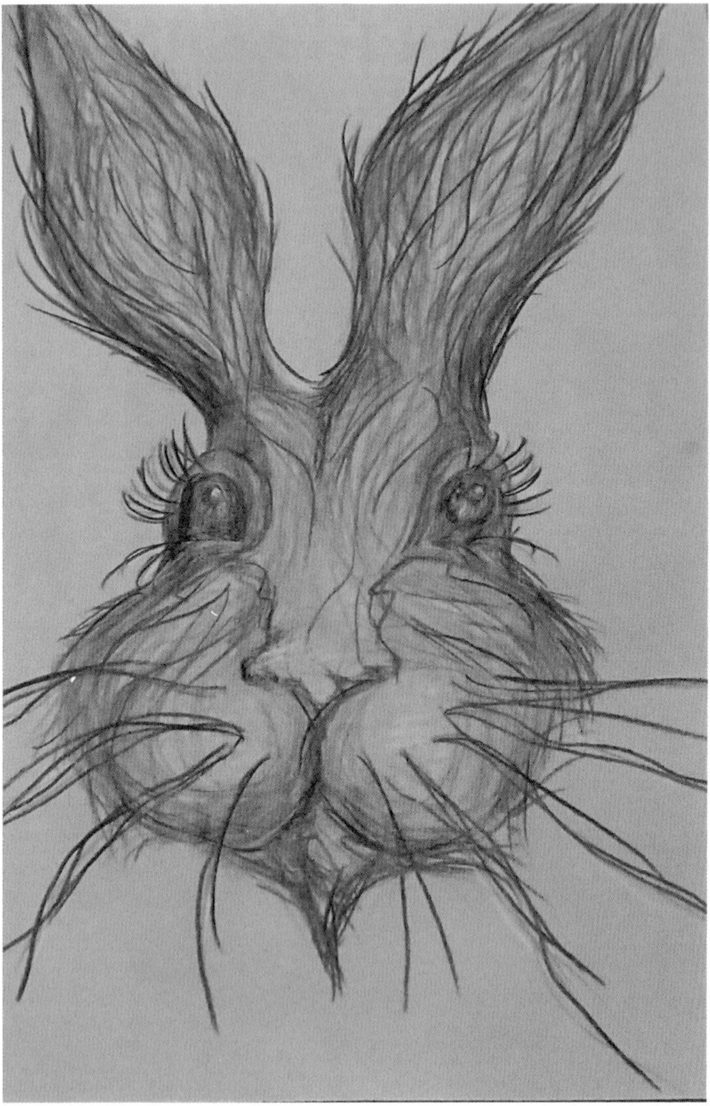

THE HARE WITH GREEN EYES

The first time it came to her she was fast asleep. She was dreaming. This in itself was unusual because dreams had become a rare event for this woman. It was like part of her mind had shut up shop, only opening occasionally to remind her just how weird the inside of her head could be.

Usually, these dreams were fuelled by physical prompts…a bad cold or maybe a very rich meal, but this evening there was no such explanation. By her standards she was feeling perfectly well, yet there it was, in her dream, looking at her. It had huge green eyes, not the muddy khaki that people so blessed optimistically called hazel; these eyes were a vivid iridescent green and yes they actually sparkled. To emphasise the disarming beauty of this creature, the magical green was outlined with ebony, darker than the darkest night, and then there were the eyelashes. Oh the eyelashes on that thing! Any woman would kill to have those. It didn't blink. It just looked at her with unswerving concentration. At first the woman found this very difficult to deal with, but, as the dream progressed she became more and more comfortable with the situation. Inexplicably, as there was no verbal communication between the two of them, she knew that this creature knew every single thing there was to know about her. It understood her and she knew it was going to show her the way...whatever that meant.

The creature invading her sleep was a hare: a beautiful, elegant brown hare. Its eyes were by far the most outstanding feature, but all together it was quite a sight to behold. From its athletic, slender limbs to the shimmering fur that adorned its quietly powerful frame, it sat there motionless in the moonlight, just looking at her.

That night the dream didn't go much further. She woke up feeling decidedly odd. *What the hell was all that about?* The dream and that uneasy sense of puzzlement revisited her throughout the day that followed. Those eyes...she just couldn't forget how they seemed to be looking deep into her very soul and saw everything.

Not that there was a great deal for the hare to see. She had an uneventful existence. She had no career to speak of, oh she went to work, but it was purely functional; it paid the bills. She was married, had been for some time. There were no children but that was fine, she really didn't mind. No, there was nothing spectacular about this life. The only thing she knew, and the hare knew it too, was that something was missing.

She didn't tell anyone about the dream, why would she? That's all it was; a bit of over imagination and, let's face it, who would be interested? Certainly not the spouse, he'd probably mutter and then carry on with whatever he'd been doing. One sure guarantee was that whatever that was, it would be of no interest to her.

Oh they got on; they existed in a fairly amicable state. They spoke to each other every day, but they certainly didn't talk anymore; it was peaceful and she knew it could be a lot worse, so on they went, drip feeding their life together.

The hare, however, did not go away.
The next night it returned, just looking at her with that disarming intensity of gaze before eventually bounding away to where, she did not know. The same thing happened the following night and the night after that. In a subtle way the hare's demeanour changed and the woman felt it. Still it was silent, but behind her eyes, for it was undoubtedly female, the woman could sense a pleading and a longing. For what she had no clue. This was the puzzle.

She kept her counsel and resolutely said nothing to anyone about the continual nocturnal disturbances. That said, the seeds of worry had started to take root in her mind. *What if it's a brain tumour?*

What if I'm just going mad? In spite of these anxious thoughts, a stronger fear kept her away from the Doctor's office. It was almost as if doing nothing about it meant it wasn't really happening.

Outwardly she carried on life as she had always done. No one looking at her would think for one minute that she was in any way troubled. She went to work when she was supposed to and she did her job competently. She'd never really been invested in what she did for a living; in reality she knew this meant she was not trying that hard… a steady 75% of her true capacity. It got her by and that was all that was needed. Since the hare had entered her life, she knew that she wasn't even doing *that* much; 50% on a good day. Her mind just wasn't on the job. The strange thing was, no one noticed. Not a word was said, but she could feel herself slowly and surely becoming obsessed by the creature. If she saw a picture of a hare or an ornament depicting the animal in full March madness, she bought it. The house started to look like a hare rescue facility, but still not a word was said by her husband or anyone else to question her behaviour. It was like what was happening was completely normal or, worse, that no one actually cared.

Night after night the dreams continued until it seemed she couldn't remember what life was like without the presence of the hare. It began to consume her so that the importance of what went on in her waking life started shrinking and all that mattered were the moments when she could sleep and dream. The intensity of the dreams increased as time went on. The pleading in those green eyes became more compelling to the point of seeming feverish, almost desperate.

When the animal moved, in the moonlit field she assumed was its home, it danced and jumped and it ran with so much energy and with a joy that was palpable. She wanted to reach out and touch it. Truth be told, she wanted to *be* the hare. That thought scared her, but if she was truly honest it thrilled her too.

This strange relationship with this animal, which she *knew* could only be a figment of her imagination, went on for weeks, months. Then, as springtime approached, strange became stranger, if such a thing could be possible.

She woke up after another night in the company of the hare and went through her usual routine pretty much on autopilot, as her waking life had become: a visit to the toilet, then a quick functional shower. It was then that she noticed it. There, on her right thigh, about as big as a mobile phone, lay a tattoo: a beautiful, intricate tattoo of the hare! She felt her head spin when she saw it. It was like the taps had been switched to cold as dizziness and panic nearly swept her feet from under her. She steadied herself and forced herself to look down at her thigh. It was still there. But it couldn't be real. She had never had any interest in "body art" and quite frankly would be the last person ever to get a tattoo. It was there though, she couldn't deny it. How it had arrived was a complete mystery. Then she thought about *him*... *God he's going to go ape!* Her spouse hated tattoos, especially on women; he called them "tramp stamps." *How am I going to explain this?* The panic felt very real even though she knew the tattoo couldn't be.

He was still in bed. It was Saturday, so no work for either of them, and he always took the opportunity to have a lie in, although she never could. All reason and good sense had left her at this point; she had no idea how she was going to explain it and certainly couldn't hide it, so she calmly walked into the bedroom and carried on getting ready for the day ahead. He was awake by now, but still in bed. She dropped her towel. This, even on a normal day, would not have provoked a reaction; they had been married way too long for that. But today she had the hare in all its glory, charging with gay abandon up her thigh!

He didn't bat an eyelid. She found this more disturbing than the spontaneous tattoo she now possessed. *That's it,* she thought, *it's me. I'm going bloody crazy. It's all in my head!* The thought of that terrified her more than anything. She didn't want him having her sectioned so, giving the performance of her life, she got herself dressed and their day continued, just as many other Saturdays had before.

She was surprised that sleep came to her so readily that night but it did, and of course the hare was there to meet her in this dream world where it ran and played freely. Except this night, as well as the usual pleading, there was a definite twinkle in the creature's eye. This hare was more than capable of mischief, it would seem…

When she awoke the next day she half expected the tattoo to have vanished but it remained, like it was and always had been part of her. It really was quite a spectacular piece of work. Each hair on its body had definition and almost moved when she did. The eyes had a realism and living light deep within them to the extent that she would not have been surprised if they had winked at her given the opportunity. If it had been real, and she had to keep reminding herself it just couldn't be, the artist who did it must have had an amazing gift; its intricacy and size surely meant it would have hurt like hell. It didn't hurt and this was further proof, as if she needed it, that it was a figment of her very disturbed mind.

He still hadn't said anything about it either. *This will pass,* she thought. *Whatever the imbalance in my head is has got to settle soon and I am going to wake up one morning and find it gone…*except it didn't go.

She was left to her own devices that day. He had a standing arrangement with his cronies to play golf on a Sunday and this usually meant she was on her own at least until late afternoon. The attractions of the 19th hole seemed more and more irresistible to him of late. She didn't mind too much, she'd always been comfortable with her own company; but hang on, she was never really alone these days…she had the hare.

They lived in a nice house, she couldn't complain about that, everything she wanted, in a semi- rural area with a farmer's field backing on to the bottom of her well-tended garden. Partly to distract herself, she took to the housework with almost military precision. Not a speck of dust was allowed to remain on the legion of hare ornaments that now shared her home. The place hummed with the comforting aroma of beeswax, because in all honesty she had been polishing like a bit of a maniac. It was worth it though; a house to be proud of…at least for a while before he came home and messed it up again later.

She turned her attention to outdoors. It was a lovely spring day in the middle of March. It felt like the year was finally coming to life again after the slow creeping death of winter had been forced to release its icy grip. The grass seemed greener somehow; bulbs were poking their heads cautiously above the parapet and taking a chance on sharing their blooms. Best of all it was warm enough to put the washing out.

Even she had to admit the amount of joy this routine chore brought her was disproportionate to say the least. She just loved hanging washing out to dry. It was a ritual to her. She *had* to have matching pegs for each item and the clothes *had* to be fixed to the line in a way which was aesthetically pleasing to her. *God, analyse that! No wonder I'm having hare hallucinations, I'm decidedly odd*, she thought. However, it harmed no one and made her happy and that was all that mattered.

She was in the middle of her Zen laundry ritual when something caught her eye at the bottom of the garden. Not one, but two hares sat stock still, looking right back at her! She had reached the point where nothing surprised her anymore. It actually wasn't that unusual to see wildlife thereabouts, it was semi-rural after all. What was unusual to the casual onlooker, and most of all to her, was that one of the hares had iridescent green eyes! The other one had pale grey eyes and both of them stared at her intently. She wasn't scared, just curious now, so she carefully dropped her washing and walked slowly toward them. She managed to get about ten feet away from them before they turned tail and ran off. This was enough time for her to be certain that she had met at least one of them before.

That night she almost couldn't wait to go to bed and get to sleep. Then she momentarily panicked: *What if it doesn't come?* The thought of that was unbearable. She needn't have worried. The hare came back and it brought its friend. The other hare was very different to its companion, the eyes being the most obvious feature. They were pale grey, almost silver. The animal was definitely bigger and more muscular than the other creature and she knew with absolute certainty that this one was a male.

That night her dream was more vivid than anything she had seen previously. It was night time, as it always was in the dream-world inhabited by the hares, and the sky was adorned with a galaxy of stars bigger than she had ever imagined could exist. They seemed to embrace and caress the full moon, which shone on the field that the hares called home and where they played together. Oh how they played! They jumped to impossible heights like they were coiled springs released to their absolute full potential. The woman could feel the excitement and the electricity they generated together. In the case of the male hare she could see it in his eyes which transformed from silver to midnight blue, endlessly reflecting the myriad of stars above him. She knew he wanted to be with the other creature more than life itself and she wished more than life itself that she could feel that way too...about *anything*.

It was almost as if the hares simultaneously heard her thought, her wish, in the split second it took to flash through her mind. They stopped and both of them looked deep into her heart and at last she heard the words she had wanted to hear all along....*You can.*

In the morning he woke up. The house was a mess, but that suited him; it was how he liked it, he only had himself to please. He couldn't remember his wife. It was like she had never existed: no clothes, no make-up, no ornaments, and no matching laundry on the line outside. He didn't report her disappearance because he hadn't noticed she had gone or ever been there in the first place. They had new starters in work because there was a big job on. No one noticed her desk was not occupied. They were far too busy. It was just a desk. Someone will sit at it.

Her family thought nothing of it. They'd stopped exchanging Christmas cards years ago, that was as close as they had ever been. If they had met each other at a wedding or a funeral there would have been a mutually awkward struggle to remember each other's names.

That night the moon reflected brilliantly upon the farmer's field, just as it had always done and would continue to for all eternity. In the field, *three* hares danced. They moved with more joy, abandon and freedom than they ever had before and the galaxy of stars in the midnight sky smiled upon them, illuminating their happiness. A place for everything and everything was finally in its place.

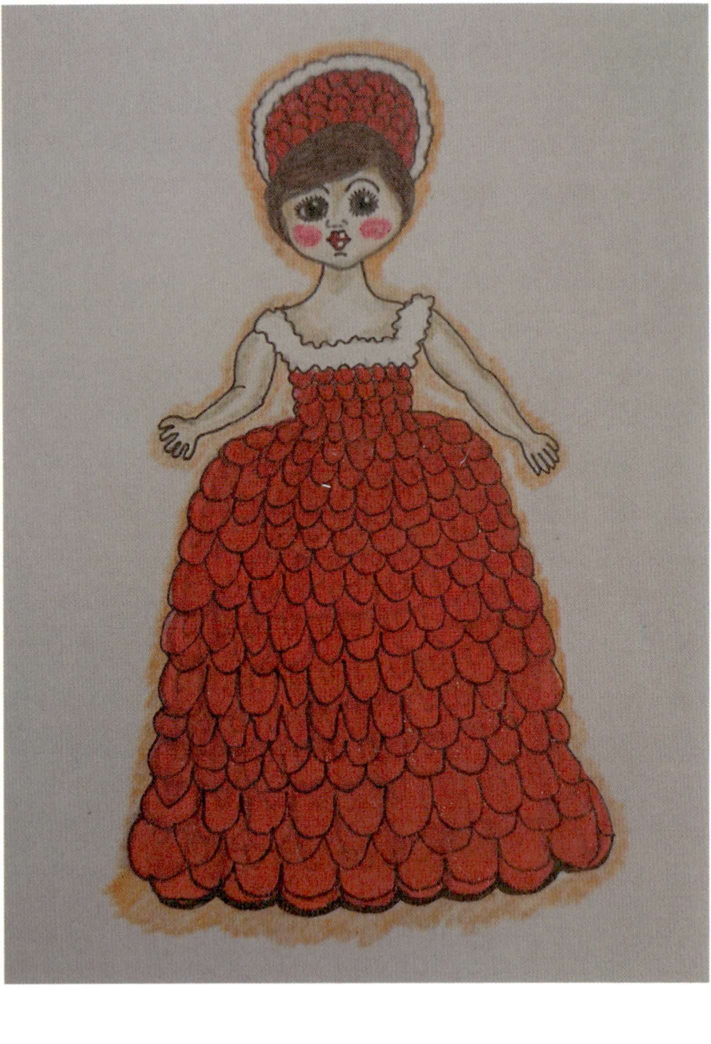

THE HOUSE WITH THREE FLOORS

Great Auntie Flo was unique. She was in *our* family anyway. It's not an exaggeration, just a simple fact. If someone said to me *sorry, our mistake, it seems baby Flo was switched at birth…these things happen,* I'd readily accept it. Don't get me wrong, there was nothing wrong with my other relatives, it was just that she was *so* very different.

Hard to believe I know, but I come from a very working class, very rough and ready family. Great Auntie Flo was the eldest of six. This family liked a drink and liked to F and blind and fight with one another: but not our Auntie Flo. She was a lady and spoke with a cut glass accent, like Celia Johnson in Brief Encounter. Received Pronunciation they call it. I'm convinced she could have worked for the BBC. The odd thing was, nobody ever questioned why she spoke that way, where it came from. This was Flo… just the way she was.

It wasn't like she was rich, but clearly she had done better for herself than the others because she had a house. Not a flat or a maisonette rented off the Corpy, her own house that she owned with Uncle Jim.

A three storey house.

It terrified me.

When my mum took me to visit, we'd stand outside the black front door waiting for it to open and I'd tell myself, *whatever you do don't look up, do not look up!* What could be looking back at me? Surely just three rows of windows, the sills painted black, the nets crisp and clean. But what if those curtains twitched? What if there was a pair of eyes I didn't recognise glaring back at me? I was never brave enough to test this theory.

Auntie Flo was exotic, she had two pets! We lived in a flat, strictly no animals allowed, or so mum told me. The nearest I got was a pyjama case that bore a passing resemblance to a poodle. Auntie Flo had a German shepherd called Flash who was always flinging itself at the plate glass window in the vestibule door, possibly, on reflection, in a bid to escape. She also had a Siamese, just like the cat on Blue Peter. I can't remember its name, but I do recall it just sitting there staring, like it knew a lot more than it would ever let on.

It was a cold house all year round, with impossibly high ceilings. There were rooms I never got to go into, like the front parlour. *Not a place for children my dear,* Auntie Flo would say, if she caught me glancing at it curiously. Then there were the other rooms that I dearly wished I would never have to go into and top of that list was the bathroom…on the third floor!

Trouble was, I was a little kid. Auntie Flo would feed me up with her special ham sandwiches and buckets of orange cordial and sooner or later, as our visits would invariably be a couple of hours at least, I would be squirming in my seat unable to keep still, as I fought the inescapable fact that I had to visit the toilet. My mum would bark at me, *have you got worms!? What's to do with you? Do you need the toilet?* I'd nod sheepishly. *Well go on then for god's sake!!* It was the seventies, that's how they did childcare then.

I knew what was ahead of me.

I'd go reluctantly into the hall but I never ever looked up those stairs: the ones I had to climb to get where I desperately needed to be.

The bathroom was right at the top of three terrible endless flights. With my eyes staring intently into the yellow and black nauseous pattern of the stair carpet, I would launch myself upwards. I'd go as quickly as I could, although the nearer I got to the top it seemed to me that the carpet was made of treacle; my feet were reluctant to go forward, like they knew what was waiting. It got colder too. Even in the height of summer. This has always bothered me. I'm no scientist, but surely heat rises right? Not here.

On this particular day, the higher I went the more it felt like I was being enveloped in an icy embrace.

I felt cold fingers tracing their dead tips along the back of my neck, not gripping me like they could, just toying with me, letting me know I was far from alone. I didn't dare turn around, even after the third time of this happening. I just kept my eyes forward.

It seemed like it took forever and that I'd never get there, but eventually I made it to the third floor. The bathroom, however, was not immediately behind a door off the landing. In fact it was nowhere near the top of the stairs. Almost like someone's idea of a very sick joke, it waited for me at the end of a very long dark and narrow corridor. I had no choice, I *had* to use the toilet! I took a deep breath, shut my eyes tightly and ran as fast as I could, hoping against hope that I would make it safely. With fingertips stretching out behind me, I propelled myself at the bathroom door, painted black of course, and stumbled through.

I had to prioritise. I had a pressing reason for putting myself through all of this after all. As I sat on the throne, I briefly forget my recent terrors and took in my surroundings. The bathroom always reeked of Paraffin because a heater was permanently holding court, belching out its noxious fumes, as it desperately tried to bring the temperature up to a level fit to sustain life.

It never succeeded.

The black tiles and the black bathroom suite were an interesting design choice. I don't think I've ever seen anything like that since. They set off Auntie Flo's collection of dolls, the type very popular in the 1970's. They had knitted skirts that covered up a never ending supply of toilet rolls and a small army of them inhabited the long black windowsill. As I stared, the eyes of the doll nearest to me fluttered slowly downwards until they were closed. The more I looked at them the more I wondered, *who's looking at who?* I closed my eyes in fear and focused on the job in hand.

Of course, after thirty seconds, my eyes inevitably returned to the window sill. The closest doll's eyes remained stubbornly shut. I focused on the window behind them, which was in a permanent state of condensation, with rivulets perpetually running like tears down its length. The longer I looked, the more organised the water trails would become. Almost hypnotised, I stared and stared until words started to form before me. It was like an invisible finger was guiding the strokes. Each letter began to take shape before my terrified eyes, until I could clearly see a sentence that read: *Go, go now!* To my horror, at the same time, every pair of hideous dolls' eyes snapped open on the windowsill until they were all staring hatefully in my direction!

Clearly I had outstayed my very limited welcome. I felt the panic rise within me. Maybe the bathroom wasn't the safe haven I'd hoped for, maybe I'd walked right into the trap that had been intended for me all along. I didn't wait long enough to find out. Running blindly back down that awful claustrophobic passageway, I made my escape and my rapid descent to safety.

I stumbled back into the kitchen and it was like they had hardly noticed I'd been away. Eventually, through a cloud of cigarette smoke, mum said to me, *did you fall down the toilet or what?* While I'd been gone, Auntie Floe had conjured up another loaf full of ham sandwiches and another glass of orange cordial. She tipped me the wink while she listened intently to mum's many grievances about the rest of our family.

I never told my mum or anyone else about the terrors I felt in that house. I thought if I did then that would make it somehow more real. Let's face it, I was a precocious child. My mum told me this often enough. I had an over active imagination, everyone always says this about me, it must be true. I was just being a daft kid, it was a sugar rush. I forgot and I grew up.

Many years later, Auntie Flo was facing her final days. She was a ripe old age by anyone's standards.

It seemed a life time of smoking and social drinking in moderation really hadn't done her any harm at all. She was queen in residence at a rather nice nursing home in Garston and I wanted to see her. I had an almost desperate need to do so. I had a feeling it was going to be the last time. Her eyes still sparkled, glinted almost, as she stared at me. Her last words will never leave me...*Silly girl. They liked you. They only wanted to play.*

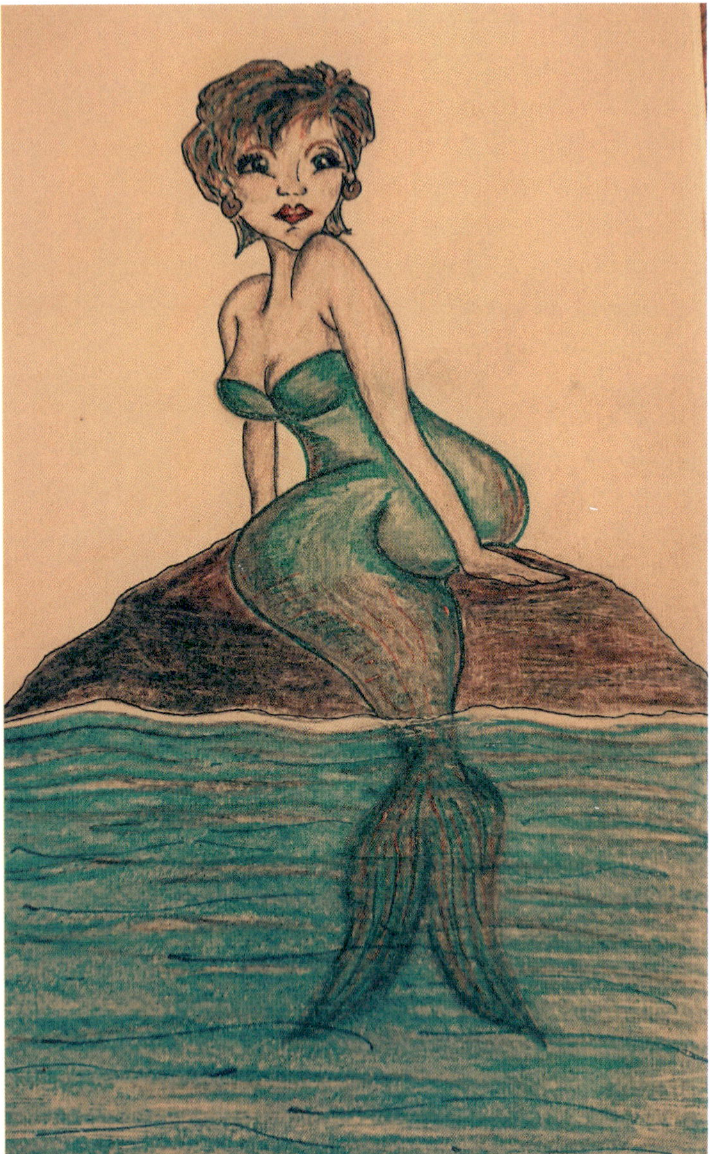

A MERMAID IN THE RIVER ALT

Have you ever seen a drunken mermaid? It's not a pretty sight believe me. They are by nature creatures of excess, so when they party, they party hard and unfortunately, even for mermaids, sometimes there are consequences.

Mairin was a mermaid of a certain age, she was still a beauty, for their beauty never fades, in fact some would say the addition of years enhanced their appeal to us mere mortals. They had a certain knowing quality that sparkled in their eyes, which were a startling green blue, not unlike the waters of the Aegean Sea.

They never knew a wrinkle or a line on their shimmering skin, far too well hydrated for that, and their hair would always catch the kisses of the sunlight as they reclined languorously on any available rock that met their approval.

Mairin was unusual. She didn't fit the stereotypical image most of us have of her kind. This was mainly to do with her hair; it was short and spiky, very chic actually, but nothing like a mermaid. It didn't drape over her shoulders or down her back. It certainly didn't cover her best assets, she was Mairin, her name meant Goddess of the Sea and she did not hide her spectacular form away from anyone, mortal or immortal.

Her skin had an aquatic luminosity, changing colour in a subtle and very beautiful way, depending on whether she was in or out of the water. She was truly enchanting without a doubt.

Mairin's favourite colour was green. Unsurprisingly really, as this was the colour of her magnificent tail and she had opted, over the passage of many hundreds of years, to cover her torso in a beautiful seamless corset that accentuated her allure to men *and women* more than her naked form ever could. A further benefit of age you see. Wisdom. She knew what mortals wanted and she knew how to make them want her…sometimes with lethal consequences.

However at 6am that morning she felt a long way from the alluring siren she was born to be. It had been a heavy night. There had been a gathering in the Irish Sea. An aquatic rave if you will. Norwegian sailors, probably the most hard-core to sail the seven seas, had been involved and let's just say…let's leave it at it didn't end well.

In short, Mairin had allowed herself to be swept

away on a tidal wave of hedonism and that is why she found herself the following morning quite literally up Shit Creek.

That's actually a bit unfair, it wasn't Shit Creek at all, it was The River Alt.

The River Alt flows North East through Lancashire and Merseyside. It rises in Huyton and flows through Croxteth Park and Maghull before tumbling out into the River Mersey.

The Alt really is a river with ideas above its station. The casual onlooker would say that most of the time it was a stream at best, at worst a drainage ditch, full of brown run off from the surrounding fields. Occasionally a spell of bad weather would inflate its meagre banks, but even then its credentials as a river in the proper sense teetered on the edge of reality.

It was a week or two of foul summer weather that had contributed in part to Mairin's predicament. It had rained virtually non-stop and, as she had drifted, completely off her gills, the tide and the wind and perhaps Fate had guided her up river, right into the net of an unsuspecting slumbering angler.

This was one of the worst possible fixes for a mermaid to find herself in. It's just not right; they have to have the upper hand at all times, especially when dealing with mortals. Finding herself stuck fast in a keep net purchased from Carp Central was Mairin's worst nightmare.

Fortunately, Fate did not have it completely in for her. Her captor was fast asleep and blissfully unaware that he had the catch of a lifetime. Actually she was probably the luckiest mermaid alive that morning because it also happened to be a full moon.

The power of the moon is immense, but did you know that it's not just the tide, gravity and Werewolves who benefit? When the moon is waxing full, mermaids have the opportunity, should they feel the need, to temporarily replace their tail with a pair of shapely legs. This allows them to roam terra firma and create a little havoc with mortal men before returning to their watery haven when the moon begins to wane.

Today the moon would save Mairin's scales. A quick wriggle and she replaced her tail with green trousers, Primark's finest, to match her corset. Her skin, while still flawless and unlined, adopted a more mortal hew to which she added a little contouring for regional authenticity. She drew the line at a Scouse brow and lip fillers…even mermaids have standards.

The wriggle was enough to wake her captor.

Ryan was the laziest and most inept angler you could possibly meet. He literally had all the gear and no idea. He'd never ever caught a fish, but that didn't matter, it got him out of the house and that made him happy.

Ryan was just into his forties, but even he would admit he looked a lot older. He was ten years married and the wife had let herself go, though he'd never dare tell her, and he was bored. Not enough to do anything about it, too lazy and they had two kids after all, but he felt the only way he could really relax was to be out of that house as much as possible: angling, shifts and pub…when she let him.

Ryan was in the middle of a rather wonderful dream involving him and the Welsh girl off The One Show when he felt the net wriggle. He tumbled unwillingly out of his slumber and nearly joined Mairin in the water.

"Jesus! Shit! Oh my God love, are you alright?!!"

Clever mermaid as she was, Mairin emulated his scouse accent. "Do I fucking look alright soft shite?! I was at a wedding last night at Croxteth Hall, pissed admittedly, but Christ knows how I landed in here. Do you think you could help me out…Please?"

"Oh shit yeah, yeah of course girl."

Funny how he called her girl. Though obviously beautiful, she did look older than him, *if only he knew how old,* but it didn't stop him noticing her eyes, in fact he couldn't stop himself from staring, looking her up and down quite thoroughly as he helped her scramble up the bank.

"Shall I call an ambulance, can I take you to A+E, are you ok, are you injured?"

She smiled at him, which given her present circumstances he wasn't expecting. "No I'm fine love, just a bit wobbly on me pins at the moment. Tell you what, if you could give me a lift to Crosby beach, you know, where the iron men are, that would be great. I don't live far from there."

As the woman had just been in his fishing net, he felt he could only agree. She borrowed his fleece to dry off and they got into his life-battered Ford Focus parked a short distance away. It was filthy; the kids owned the back seat which was littered with their toys and mountains of fast food detritus. The smell of it almost made Mairin hurl; she was only saved from this by the heady aroma of the man. Mermaids are highly sensitive to testosterone, it attracts them to mortals like moths to a flame. This Ryan wasn't such a bad example really, she pondered, he certainly had it over a few of those Norwegian fishermen from the night before. She noticed he had tattoos, they were always a plus in her book...but that stench of...she could barely think the word...FAMILY...that pervaded the vehicle stopped her from doing something, and there's no point in modesty here, that Ryan would never have forgotten.

"Plenty more fish in the sea," she thought as he dropped her off at Crosby promenade.

"Are you sure this is ok love?" he said, seemingly reluctant to leave. Don't judge Ryan, this wasn't his fault. Even when she wasn't trying to ensnare a man, just being in her company for a short time was enough to become enchanted by her.

"Oh I'm fine, I'm only over there," she replied, waving vaguely towards the water. "You need to get home…your wife and kids will be wondering where you are."

This was enough to jump start Ryan back to reality: he panicked. No way was he going to be able to explain this one to the wife without there being absolute murder. He quickly formulated a diversionary tactic of a full Mackies breakfast for everyone, then she wouldn't even notice his fleece was dripping wet. She'd be too busy shovelling her hash-browns, and his too, into her gob.

As his car disappeared into the distance, Mairin wandered over to a bench and made herself as comfortable as her temporary legs would allow. She waited for the moon to rise and the turning of the tide.

Eventually, the promenade was absent of all mortal life and the waxing moon was high in the night sky. Mairin approached and sat on the sea wall, which was being roughly caressed by the rising waves. Her Primark trousers and her mortal legs vanished, only to be replaced by her glorious lustrous tail. Her iridescent skin glittered seductively under the light of the moon and stars and she gasped, "Ahh…at last," as she disappeared below the surface.

She wasn't alone in the water. A colony of rather judgemental mermen, who had taken to skulking in the guise of being "iron men" when the tide was low and the moon was full, tut tutted as she swam elegantly past.

"Maybe go easy on the Norwegian sailors next time Mairin," one of them called, as her bubble trail faded into the distance. Her laughter echoed loud and long into Liverpool Bay, to the Mersey Bar and beyond.

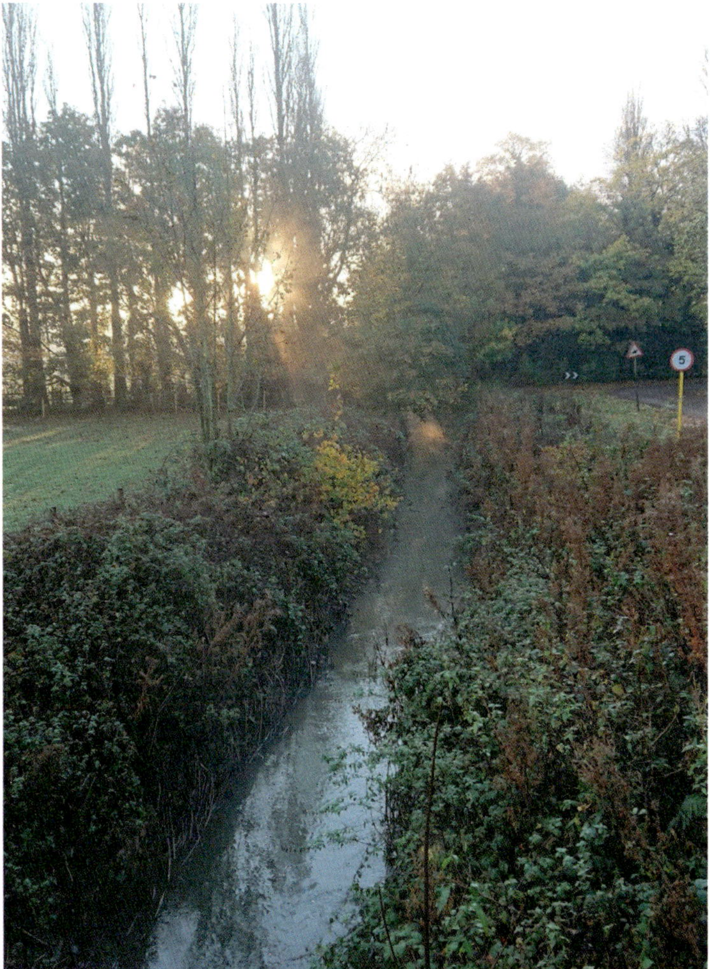
5

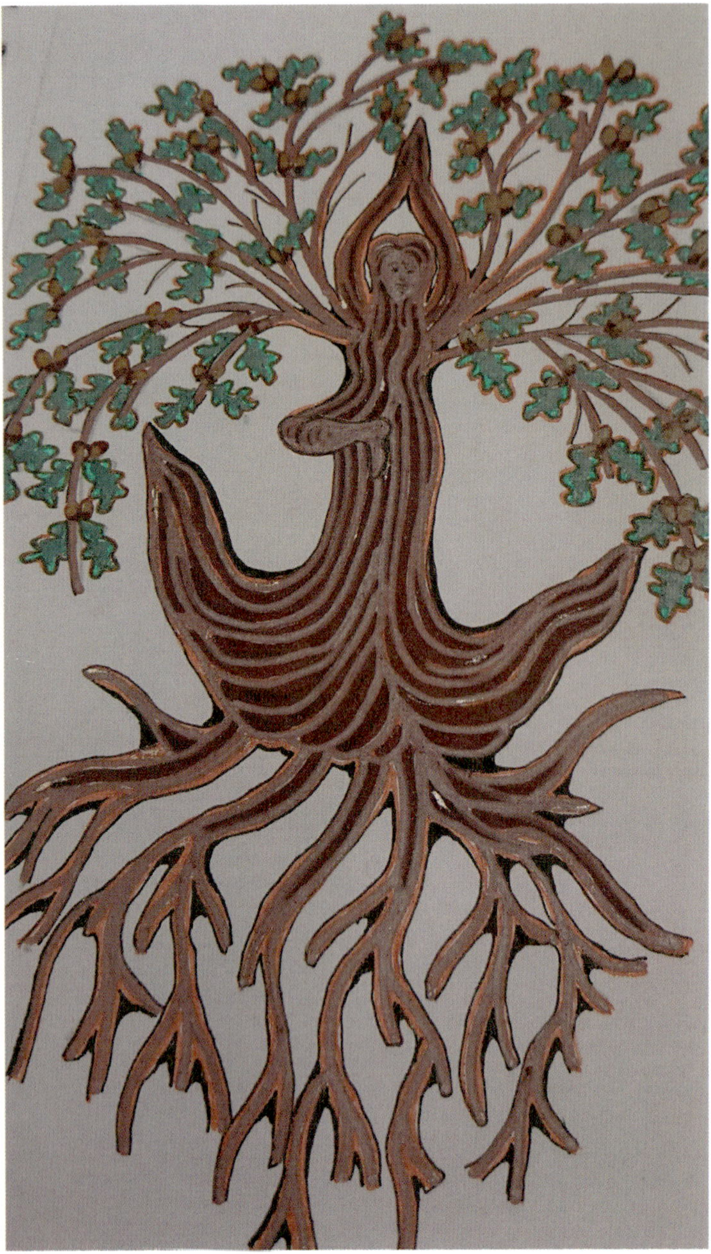

THE MUSINGS OF AN ANCIENT OAK

A tree is just a tree…right?

You should *never* ask a lady her age. In any event I wouldn't know where to begin. I don't subscribe to years; they are nothing more than meaningless numbers to me, a tool for humankind to record the passage of time. I see the changing of the seasons and this is only right and proper: tangible segments, each prompting an action in my existence. I may have no eyes, but don't be mistaken, I see and I feel all that is around me as my beautiful green knuckles tightly grip the earth. My roots spiral deeply beneath, extending further than is possible for you to imagine and they anchor and sustain me against the wild winds that will occasionally have the audacity to shift me from my chosen spot. They never succeed.

I suppose if you were scientifically inclined you could always count my rings but really…how vulgar, how invasive…I mean, I barely know you! Let's just settle on this fact. I am ancient. Vintage. I have observed and felt all that I survey for generations.

You only have to look at me now, resplendent in my springtime glory and it's clearly obvious. My trunk is shapely with a commanding girth. I stand firm and resolute. My branches are melodic in their form as they spiral skywards and are abundantly adorned with fresh new green leaves, not a line, wrinkle or blemish to be seen. I dare you to find one. This is my favourite time. I am at my peak. I feel young again, newly rejuvenated, a sapling, giddy with the promise of what lies ahead, eager to see who will pass me by and add to my collection.

I get them all here. People, I mean. Hardly surprising, as I am planted on a pathway incising a country park, once an ancient woodland barely occupied by humanity but now a busy thoroughfare for leisure. They love me. What's not to love? It must be my welcoming nature. Some have actually taken to flinging their bony little limbs around me and hugging me! I'm not complaining, they do me no harm, apart from the occasional dog using me as a toilet. It's as though they feel my warmth, my great age and my wisdom; I suppose it must seep out of me, a liquid kiss like the sap that rises up within my branches. I can't help it, it's just the way I'm made, but really I give *nothing* up to them. Oh no, I'm a collector. I'm the keeper of their secrets and they don't even know they are giving them to me.

I'm the ultimate people watcher. Let's face it, I've

been doing this for hundreds of years, looking on impassively as generations pass me by. Nothing really changes, apart from me of course. I just get better and better. People though? Let's just say they haven't evolved a great deal.

It's the couples I *really* like to watch closely. Men and women, now more often men with men or girls with girls. I don't care. Whatever rings your bell. They are *all* so interesting in their own way. Some are open with their feelings, the older couples linking or even hand in hand as they stroll past. They, like me, are examples of vintage at its best. I feel their love and I keep a little for myself. Call it my finder's fee. Honest and faithful, steady, true. Boring you say? Perhaps to some, but they are hurting no one.

Then there are the others.

To the casual onlooker everything is fine, but I feel so much more than they can ever see. The couples who talk, or worse who are silent, as they stare into the middle distance, the pain behind their eyes burning into their souls while they try their best to make everything look normal and yet…they just exist. Nothing more.

Surrounded by natural beauty, some of them would rather walk, head bowed, engrossed by the empty contents of their telephone. They have my pity as they pass me by. I take nothing from them and their kind. I don't need that negative energy.

Best of all are the lovers. I can feel a crackle of life, and often lust, between them - sparks of light that only I am able to discern. I feel what *they* feel and it's delicious. Perhaps it's the freshness of the prospect of a new love, a conquest or, even better, something a little more illicit. Sometimes naughty can be very nice let me tell you; I don't judge and I certainly do like to be entertained and energised by their furtive excitement, whatever the reason. I suppose this makes me sound like something of a voyeur. Do I look like I care? Just leave a little of that feeling behind and I'll be satisfied.

My favourite time of day is when the dawn breaks and the birds who share the woodland with me release their voices into the air, waking the earth up with their glorious melody. A summer morning, perhaps a little chilly, when the sunshine paints all before it with its golden light and the spiders' webs that adorn my branches are suddenly bejewelled by countless sparkling droplets. We all need a little glamour you know.

Sadly, the excitement of spring and the dizzy heat of summer are but fleeting moments. I revive, I flourish and then…I begin to fade. My leaves, relentlessly harassed by the summer breezes, forget their zest and begin to fracture. Like brittle old women. Autumn sneaks up on me and tries to take advantage of my delicate state but, I'm sorry, I don't tolerate decay. I drop those leaves like discarded friends; I give up my acorns like ungrateful children, casting them off my branches with no hint of regret. I'm a lover betrayed and I don't take that well. Let the toddlers in their wellies kick them along the floor as they dance through the ever shortening days that herald the arrival of winter.

How do I maintain my beauty? Sleep, of course. As winter replaces autumn, it steals the daylight away from me and lulls me into a season of slumber, caressing my form with its icy hands. I don't fear it, I welcome the rest and, don't forget, I've got my collection to keep me warm.

Next time you take a woodland walk, look around you; see the beauty and wisdom in front of your eyes and, above all, never think that a tree is just a tree.

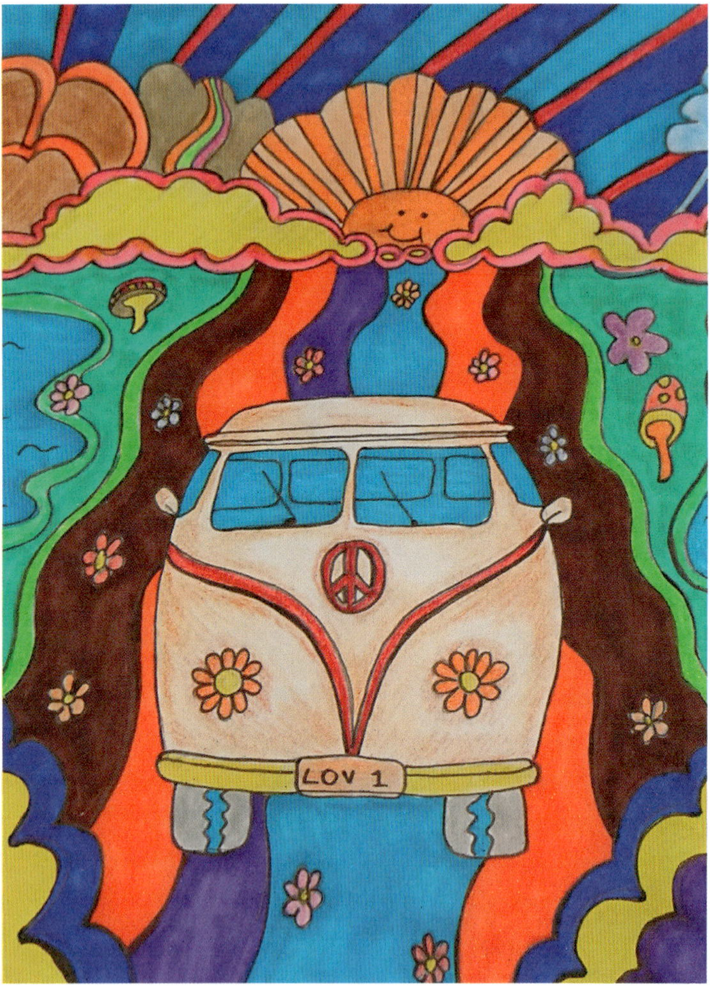
LOV 1

ALWAYS READ THE SMALL PRINT

The notion of a camper van holiday has always appealed but I'd always managed to talk myself out of it. Too cramped! Too uncomfortable! Let's face it... I'm a bit of a princess; it's just not posh enough! Decades of five star holidays all over the world had fizzled out my ambition to "hit the road man" like some long discarded joss stick. My comfort is too precious.

That was until Lockdown.

Twelve weeks is a long time to think about the future, whatever that was going to be. One thing was crystal clear: the holidays of my past, travelling thousands of jet miles to be pampered within an inch of my life, were going to be consigned to rose-tinted history. If I wanted a holiday, and I did more than anything, I was going to have to look closer to home. Unfortunately everyone else had the same idea and staycations in the UK were expensive and as rare as hen's teeth.

Anyone who knows me will tell you I'm a rather

determined type and this led me to embark on an internet search of epic proportions. It was getting disheartening, either prices were frankly ridiculous or opportunities had been snapped up by those quicker off the mark. I was beginning to get discouraged when, deep into the night with eyes red rimmed and watery from tiredness, I discovered what I thought I was looking for.

"Magical VW for hire in the UK. Fancy a trip? You know what to do."

How could I not respond to that?

Shaking with excitement, I fired off an enquiry and almost immediately a response hit the inbox. *Must be an auto response, it's 3am after all.* It wasn't. I couldn't believe my luck! Only a short drive into Cheshire, a modest fee *and* availability!

The next day I was frantically preparing for my big adventure. I had to constantly remind myself *it's only a VW camper, not a five star all-inclusive in Cancun.* I'd have to fend for myself. I'd have to travel light…Oh God, the very thought of that, but I *needed* a holiday! I needed to get away from my, albeit lovely, house: my very comfortable prison for the last twelve weeks. In spite of these very first world problems, I overcame them like the trooper I am and drove my little car, with some trepidation, to the address sent to me in the nocturnal email.

The location was not quite what I had been expecting. Rural Cheshire yes, but this place was at the end of a very long and winding lane I'd never encountered before. It was cloaked in ever denser foliage that seemed to wave me along as I drove at a steady ten miles an hour until I found myself in a somewhat dilapidated farmyard, bumper to bumper with a VW van and...a wizard. Ok, I may be exaggerating here, I don't know if he actually *was* a wizard. Let's just say the owner of the van had made the decision, a very long time ago, to opt out of mainstream society. If my dear dad was still with us he'd no doubt have said "bloody hell it's Catweasel!" I was only momentarily distracted by the wiz.., I mean the proprietor, because I was completely enchanted by the VW van. It was actually *glowing* in the summer sunshine. Painted a beautiful peach blush with iridescent red stripes, I immediately LOVED HER! Of course she was a she. No man could be that beautiful.

Her owner wore a wry smile as my delight had been impossible to conceal.

"She's a beauty. Take her anywhere you want to go. All you have to do is ask Cassandra nicely.

I was charmed by his eccentricity and I could barely wait to get behind the wheel and begin my adventure.

Wiz had other ideas.

"All *we* need to do is get the paperwork out of the way. Terms and conditions. Terms and conditions so important. Got to have your pretty little signature here."

He pointed with his hemp fabric sleeve to a rather weighty document which I swear had appeared out of nowhere. He certainly was dedicated to his theme, as even this had a hint of "Lord of the Rings" about it. The paper was quite thick parchment and the "X" at the bottom, where I was supposed to sign, had obviously been placed by a calligrapher skilled in elvish.

On reflection I *should* have read it in detail before I put pen to paper, but I was demob happy. I was free after twelve weeks indoors.

I was reckless.

After quickly scribbling my best autograph, I unpacked my car and loaded the contents into the VW.

"Safe travels," smiled Catweasel as I drove into the distance.

I was woefully unprepared for all this. Where was I going? I'd done no research or planning, this was completely off the cuff. An impulse if ever there was one. The excitement of doing something so entirely out of character, something NO-ONE would have ever expected me to do, was making me positively giddy. Yes I'd packed my SPF 30 sun cream, I'd packed my mobile phone charger *and* even remembered my phone, but I didn't have a map. The van had no sat-nav and, even if it had, I didn't want it. I was planning to follow my nose.

Until I heard the cough.

Someone, or something, inside the VW with me had coughed.

It's not like the interior of the VW is big, it's not a Tardis after all. I definitely heard a cough and it was *definitely* coming from underneath the passenger seat. As if to confirm I wasn't going mad, the cough repeated itself. If I'm honest it was a little bit staged, like a bad actor in an even worse play, but they'd achieved their objective. Whoever it was now had my attention.

This was something I couldn't deal with on the move. I pulled over into a lay-by and tentatively tipped the passenger seat forwards to find a small box with five small holes tapped into the top, quite neatly, like five on a dice. Securing the lid was an ornate little handle, almost disproportionately pretty to what it was attached to and I couldn't resist it. I carefully opened it and lifted the lid.

"At last! By the Goddess, I thought you'd never stop! I've got needs you know! Check the agreement! Go on check it!"

I've never taken an illicit drug in my life. I've never even been that drunk, I had a sheltered youth, but I could only imagine the way I felt at that precise moment was the way I would have felt if I was completely and utterly pissed. What was I looking at? How was this happening?

The owner of the voice stood before me, looking upwards with her hands on her hips and a very indignant expression on her face. No more than five inches tall, her wild green hair tumbling down her back and cocooned by an oversized cardigan, there stood before me the tiniest woman I had ever seen. She really wasn't happy…

"Don't you know what the deal is love?" She sounded exasperated.

Clearly I didn't.

"I've been waiting an eternity to get out of that farmyard… away from him…I'm sick of the sight of that lentil munching, gas producing, *boring* wizened old git! Now you, my lovely, have agreed to be my companion, my driver, my minder…Call it what you like, you're mine!"

As you can imagine, this came as something of a shock. The wiry little woman with the crazy green hair shot me a look like she knew I was unaware of what I'd signed up for.

"You will do *all* that and more because *you* signed

the paperwork. A deal is a deal. If you don't…*there'll be murder!"*

It was clear this was not an idle threat. Small as she was, I was in no doubt that she meant every syllable.

Not an auspicious start, but it seemed I really had no choice. She told me she had kinfolk in Scotland and we headed North. When we stopped for the night, I did what I should have done in the first place and read the agreement from cover to cover. It was watertight. I had signed my life away to the perpetual servitude of Cassandra. I was at her beck and call until such time as I was no longer physically able and even then I would be required to engage the services of a replacement, by fair means *or foul,* before I could be released. Old Catweasel had been quite the smartarse really, making the best of desperate times to get this tiny tyrant off his hands. All it cost him was the price of a rather swanky VW van.

Funny thing is, I'm actually rather fond of her. I've lost count of the number of weeks we've been together now, time has no meaning to me…but I know it's much more than the twelve I spent at home that's for sure and, if I'm honest, it's flown by. I have no needs, somehow the van never requires petrol, food is always in the cupboard (no lentils of course) and we never run out of money. Perfection. Apart from the underlying threat of murder and the fact that she NEVER stops yapping, I've never been happier.

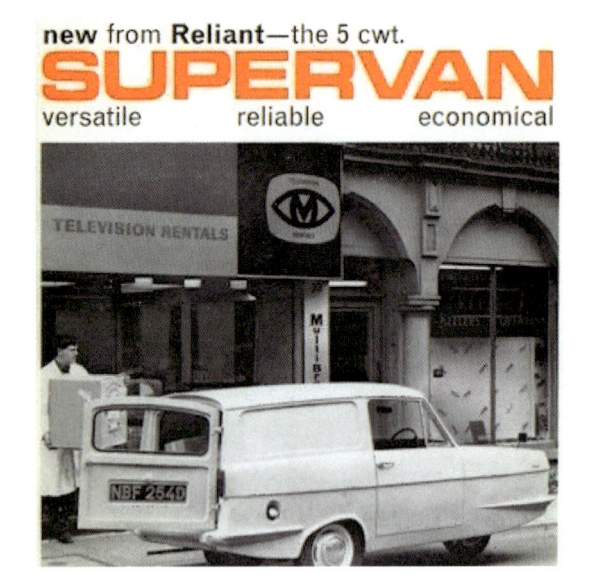

new from **Reliant**—the 5 cwt.
SUPERVAN
versatile   reliable   economical

CUT AND SHUT

My favourite film as a child was, without question, "Chitty Chitty Bang Bang." I didn't just love it, I ADORED it. Those two children in the back of that beautiful magical car...I didn't want to be them, I wanted to be their more appealing younger sister, the one who everyone loved the best. Oh what fun we'd have! Just living in the windmill house with the other two and Dick Vandyke would have done me, but a magical car too? The absolute cherry on my cake.

My cake turned out to have quite a different flavour. No windmill for me, but I wasn't deprived...I had an urban adventure playground. I grew up in a council flat tenement "city" called "Sir Thomas White Gardens" in Everton - a child of Thatcher's Britain, rather than The Home Counties. That said, I was extremely lucky in a lot of respects when I left school in 1985. I was out of work just two weeks before being offered not one but two decent jobs. I had a boyfriend *and* we even had our own car, bought in advance of him passing his test, which of course he did. Life was Truly Scrumptious indeed.

Let me tell you about that car.

Not for us a boring Ford Fiesta or a bland Vauxhall Astra. Our vehicle of choice was a Reliant Regal Supervan III costing the princely sum of £110.00. This was not a lot of money, even in 1985. We were understandably nervous as we handed over our cash to what my mum would have certainly called a "Hell's Angel." The reality was he was actually quite a friendly chap who just happened to have a leather biker's jacket and windswept long hair, just below his collar line. He was neither overtly angelic or one of Beelzebub's hordes, but he certainly did have a glint in his eye: a bit of a charming rogue.

"Alright kids, there he is. Don't let ANYONE call it a fucking Reliant Robin, it's a 1972 Reliant Regal Supervan III...emphasis on *super*; it's a flyer, quite a different beast."

We didn't really know what he was going on about, but we were not going to debate the point with him. All we knew was this decidedly dodgy three wheeled little car was going to give us our independence and we drove away happy...then we let his dad see it.

"Cut and shut that, cut and shut. Why in the name of God did you buy this heap?" He was far from impressed. Our confidence shattered, we even tried to take it back to the Hell's Angel the next day, but his yard, somewhere in the South end of Liverpool, was deserted, his phone number dead...like he'd never existed. Maybe, I speculated, my mum's unseen assessment of this man was spot on. It was a fait accompli; we were stuck with it now and decided, like we had a choice, to make the best of things.

The decision was made fairly early on that our car was a "he" not a "she." A "he" called Reg to be exact... Reg the Reliant and we were going to make him extremely handsome. My job was interior aesthetics, making sure this ancient three wheeler had a bit of style on the inside if nothing else. Reg had no back seats, he was a Supervan after all, so I made sure his fibreglass interior was as comfortable as possible. Furry seat covers for the cockpit from Motorworld, blankets and cushions from Home and Bargain, the best our money could buy, were strewn ever so precisely in the back. God help anyone who had the misfortune to be our passenger, their arse would never forgive us.

I also decided the exterior colour of our unique ride - a rather fetching teal, or some might say a turquoise blue - would hide the seams in the fibre glass if nothing else. Of course this was no professional paint job, just lots of cans of spray paint and a couple of fume filled Sundays spent in the Large Objects Store belonging to Liverpool Museum. The boyfriend's brother in law worked there and his team of very keen volunteers couldn't wait to get their sweaty hands on our little car. In particular, one called Dick was borderline obsessed with Reg. He was another one with a glint in his eye, no leather jacket this time, just an oil sodden boiler suit and an absolute certainty on my part that he'd never had a girlfriend, real or imaginary. We trusted him and by the time he was done every square inch of that car had been cleaned, refurbished and was sparkling through the toxic clouds that passed for air in that workshop.

"Just practice your double de-clutching lad and you'll be laughing…got yourself a smasher there!"

I swear he had a tear in his eye as we drove our way out of the museum car park and onward towards the open road, the 700 cc engine, sounding like a mildly irritated lawnmower, propelling us along at a steady 30 mph.

To clarify, this car was the exact same model as Del Boy's in Only Fools and Horses. You can imagine then the cracks at our expense. I like to think though that we had the last laugh in the end.

We had simple tastes back then. After a week in work, I'd rush to get home and be ready for Reg and the boyfriend to pick me up and drive us along the coast to North Wales for the weekend, where his Mum and Dad had an old but very cosy caravan. They came along too in their own car and, as we were unmarried, they made absolutely certain no hanky panky *ever* occurred! He slept at one end of the van, me at the other, while they were slap bang in the middle in the bed that folded up into the caravan wall during the day. In spite of this passion killer we *did* have fun; it's not all about sex when you're 18. We loved going to the chippy on a Friday night, going to the bright lights of Rhyl or Prestatyn on a Saturday and, in between, driving mile after mile in Reg. We discovered very early on in our ownership that this was no ordinary three wheeler.

It was the middle of summer and we decided to have a really big adventure. With a flask of tea rolling around in the back, bouncing off the special cushions like a giant pinball machine, we set off to explore the Conwy Valley beyond Betws y Coed and the mountains of Snowdonia. All looked promising…the sky was an unbelievable blue as we set off and our hearts were bursting with happiness at the prospect of a wonderful day ahead. Oh foolish youths! This was North Wales after all; the weather can change in the blink of a sheep's eye and often does.

We'd just got through the congestion of fellow scousers in Betws y Coed and were heading toward Capel Curig…quite possibly the wettest place in the UK. As if on cue, the heavens opened and rain like I have never seen before or since came hurtling down. Whatever stair rods are, it was definitely raining these.

No problem we thought, Reg will keep us dry.

He did, for about a minute, until water started rushing into the footwell and steam began to rise alarmingly as it hit the manifold!

"We're going to die!!" I wailed, ever one for being over dramatic and, frankly, unhelpful in a crisis.

"Don't be stupid!" he said, but I could see even his youthful nerve wavering as the rain got even heavier and the car began to aqua plane.

It was hard to see…Reg had very small, ineffectual wipers and they were failing to clear the windscreen. The raindrops were obscuring it like tears down the face of an inconsolable child. It seemed like we were the only car on the road now, deep in the Welsh mountains.

In the middle of nowhere.

Panic set in and I began to screech like a banshee, "Press that button! Press that button! Press it! Press it!"

"Don't be daft!" He was laughing as he said this but I knew in his own way he was bricking it.

Dick, our virgin mechanic, had (for a laugh) fitted a "turbo boost" to the dashboard. It connected to nothing…he was just taking the piss out of our car.

Ha bloody ha.

I *knew* the button was fake but I was beginning to

see my life flash in front of my eyes now. I started pressing it for all I was worth, slamming it, hoping for a miracle.

"Come on! Please! Get us out of this!"

At this point my boyfriend was probably questioning his potential life partner choices, but then his face dropped. As did mine, because we *both* felt it. The car, with us in it, was no longer travelling on the road. Reg was FLYING!

I stopped screeching at this point and as calmly as I could, with my hands gripping tightly onto the edge of my fur clad seat, said to whoever, whatever was listening, "Just get us back to the caravan, safely… please."

We came to a hover about ten feet above the sodden surface of the road and the car did a careful aerial u turn, before heading back along the mountain road. As the terrain became less rural, we could sense Reg descending gently back to earth until the three tyres confirmed it as they bounced us back onto the tarmac. It was still raining heavily. The light of the day had failed and we were lucky no one had seen our airborne escapade. The rest of the journey back to the caravan was made in a stunned silence, but we had to talk about the three legged elephant in the room. We eventually agreed that it *had* happened, we simply couldn't explain it. In spite of my deep love for all things Chitty, I knew in my heart that in reality CARS DO NOT FLY. Trouble was, we were in no position to get rid and buy another less… unpredictable vehicle. Don't forget, this was the 80's; times were hard and our earnings were far from spectacular, so Reg remained and we never spoke of the "Welsh incident" again.

As the months went on, the memory faded a little and we developed a perverse kind of pride in our ownership of this car. Yes it had zero street credibility and never would be cool, but we both knew, because we'd seen it and felt it, that Reg was somehow looking after us.

Good things and even strange things like this must come to an end. We simply had to move on and get a vehicle equipped with a back seat for our passengers. An advert was placed in the Merseymart dangling the carrot of "any reasonable offer considered." But we had to be realistic, who wanted a three wheeler in 1986?

We were surprised the very next day to get a bite from a man living in the South end of Liverpool.

"Oh yeah lad, I'm dead interested. Bring her along to my yard tomorrow and I'll have a look."

With heavy hearts, we drove Reg to an address in Garston, which, as we approached, seemed oddly familiar…then the penny dropped. It was the former home of the Hell's Angel who had sold Reg to us in the first place! I say former, I should correct that because, beaming at us as he leant against the wall, was the spawn of the Devil himself! Same jacket, same glint, just slightly longer hair.

"Has he behaved then? He's looking good lad, I'll give you that."

Slightly dumbfounded, we were dumbstruck as he counted out £220 in crisp notes into the wavering hand of my boyfriend: TWICE what we had paid for it.

"Got a really keen customer. Wants to convert him into a trike. He'll be flying before he knows it…."

Since then we've owned many cars, each one more expensive and sophisticated than the last. I've *even* seen the real Chitty Chitty Bang Bang and she made my heart sing, but nothing beats Reg. Magical, demonically possessed…you decide. Who cares, you always love your first car don't you?

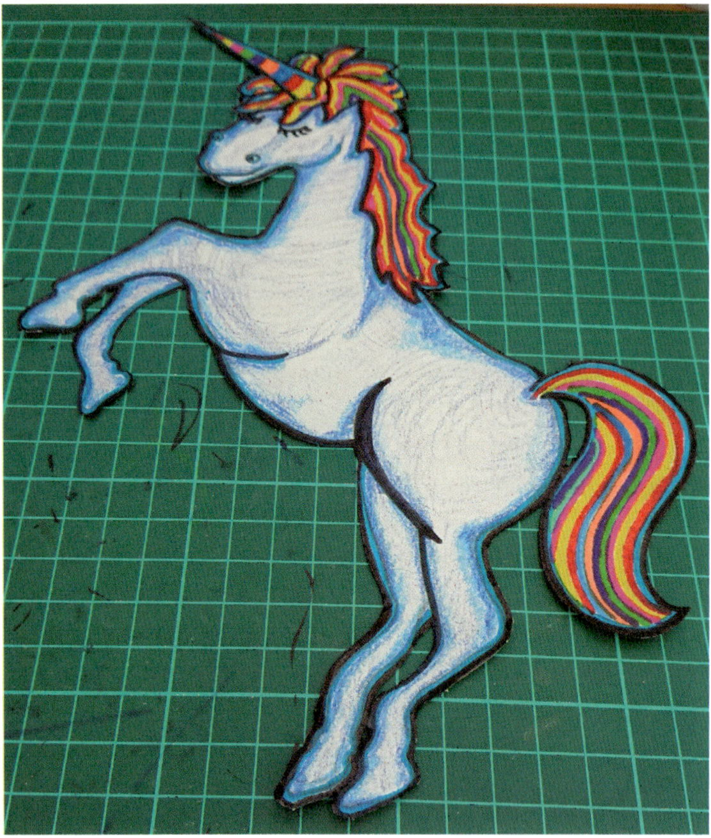

THE LAST UNICORN

Nobody knew where Blue came from. She just appeared in the field next to the riding school, along with the frost sparkling on the grass, on that bitter cold February morning.

She was all by herself and very much looked like she was really wishing she was somewhere else.

As the staff arrived to begin their day, they were at a loss when they saw her and quickly realised she had been abandoned. Who would have done such a thing? Fancy dumping this beautiful girl in their paddock!

You've probably guessed that Blue was a horse. Not just any old worn out pony, no this was a beautiful white horse. She had a glorious mane, thick and wild, that shielded her bewildered eyes, which glistened like sapphires, as the winter sun bathed the field in morning light. Hers was the body of an elite athlete. Each muscle tightly toned and tuned for performance. This was enhanced by the shading of her ice white coat, which surely must have been grey but really looked for the entire world like powder blue. It was as if a top make-up artist had been engaged to make her look as glamorous as possible and had made a really good job of it. She was a stunner. Simply gorgeous.

It was all the more surprising then that she had been abandoned. There were no instructions, no note of explanation; she was simply there. Bemused as they were by this gift-horse, the riding school staff had no option other than to take her in and give her a name. They called her Blue.

Of course, the police were notified and all the animal charities. They even put her picture on every social media platform they could think of, but to no avail. No one had reported the loss or theft of a beautiful white horse. Nobody claimed her. She seemed to be in excellent health, so why would anyone not want her? This was a strange but extremely fortunate dilemma for the owners of the riding school. While she grazed in their paddock, they had the perfect poster girl for their business.

Children and adults alike couldn't help but stare as they walked past her paddock. They were all attracted to her and why wouldn't they be? She was glorious to behold, especially in the morning sunshine. All of them wished they could ride a horse like her but they never would. You see Blue had one unfortunate fault as far as the riding school were concerned. She was a bit of a wild one. Not skittish, not feisty, she was way beyond that. She'd let the staff feed her and grudgingly even groom her, but any attempt to get on her back would be given short shrift. Her sapphire eyes would take on a steely glint and she would, as they said in those parts, *start to create*…big time! When this happened, it just wasn't safe to be around her. One swift kick from her powerful back legs and you really would know about it. An understanding was reached and Blue remained in her paddock, a solitary equine temptation, unburdened by any aspiring riders. The amount of interest she generated for the riding school was worth the cost of her food and board alone.

At least Blue didn't discriminate; she wasn't too keen on the other horses either! Similarly, the horses in the main paddock across the path just didn't want to know her. They kept their distance, more interested in catching the eye of the next group of riders, hoping to get a run out and a carrot or two. There was one exception to this: a rather dashing grey pony with handsome dapples dancing along his flanks. This besotted romantic had been trying since Blue's arrival to attract her attention with absolutely no success. At least once or twice a day he would try to engage the Prima Donna on the other side of the path in some kind of discourse. A snort, a whinny or, if he was feeling particularly frustrated, a bit of a hoof stamp or a kick in her direction. All to no avail. She gave him nothing. This grey was a persistent character and soon the stable workers couldn't help but notice his antics. They'd laugh and call him "soft lad...she'll never be your girlfriend Dob you div" and then console him with a polo mint.

Horses talk to each other. Why wouldn't they? Do you really think humans are the only creatures capable of communicating with one another? How typically arrogant of your species to believe that. Of course animals talk to each other. They are just much more selective about whom to.

Every night since Blue's mysterious arrival, the lower paddock had been awash with gossip.

"Who is she?" they would continually speculate. "The state of her, with her big mad wig...wouldn't be seen dead with a skanky mane like that!"

Sadly, jealousy is not an emotion confined to humanity alone. None of the other horses wanted to make friends with Blue. They didn't like how this stranger had disrupted their routine. This glamorous interloper had effortlessly stolen the attention away from them and this was unforgivable. That was with the exception of Dob, the love struck grey. He *really* wanted to know this stunning girl but she was still having none of it. She would look right through him as if he wasn't there...or was it as if *she* wanted to be somewhere else? This didn't stop him having a nightly chat with her - very one sided of course. During these one way conversations, Dob, as the weeks trotted by, revealed quite a bit about himself to his uninterested audience of one.

"Before you came it was me they picked on, you know? They still do a bit but I think they find you way more interesting. You're a novelty, that's for sure"

Not a flicker from the paddock across the path.

"Do you know what they call me?" It wasn't a rhetorical question. "Dobbin the Rocking horse! Just because of my markings! I can't help it; it's the way I'm made. I'm a real horse though, not a pony or a child's toy!" You could tell the other horses had clearly struck a nerve with their teasing. "I hate it. I'm never going to be Black Beauty…I'm just going to be me."

For once Blue looked like she was actually taking notice of what he'd said. As if to prove it, she took a deliberate, graceful stride to the fence which encircled her paddock and looked at him intensely with a purposeful glint in those midnight blue eyes.

"Pure jealousy hun. You are special and unique and don't you forget it….A bit like me, but not quite as spectacular!" And with that she gave a dramatic toss of her mane before trotting off to the other side of her paddock. Conversation over.

Dob was left gobsmacked, but so happy that he could feel his head spinning with excitement. At last it seemed like he had a friend.

These unlikely companions continued their, mainly one sided, conversations over the weeks that followed. Dob was definitely the mouthpiece of the partnership, chattering away every night, while Blue half listened contentedly as she continually looked into the distance, seemingly scanning the horizon for whatever it was that was missing in her life. Dob didn't mind. In fact he'd never been happier. He didn't care about what the other horses thought of him either because it didn't matter. He knew he was special, just like Blue.

He tended not to ask any direct questions of Blue because there was a fairly good chance she would give him one of her looks by way of response and, without saying a word, make him feel just a little bit foolish. However, on a warm summer's evening around the middle of May, he couldn't stop himself.

"Blue, what's that in your mane? It looks for all the world like colours…almost like a rainbow."

Blue did something then that Dob had never seen her do before; she smiled at him with her mesmerising eyes and he knew immediately that this smile came straight from her heart.

"You've noticed it then. If it looks like a rainbow then it must be a rainbow mustn't it scone-head?" This was said in a kindly way, she wasn't mocking him like the other horses would have done. "Have you not clocked me tail too?" He hadn't. He looked and was amazed to see ribbons of colour shimmering and dancing through her very long tail as the moon began to rise in the summertime sky.

"I have a secret," she said dramatically.

"No kidding? Who did that to you and why did you let them?" This was a very brave outburst from Dob, knowing Blue's temperament, but he was confident enough in their friendship that he could risk it. Blue got as close as she could to Dob from her side of the path and said very deliberately

"I'm not a horse."

Have you ever seen a horse laugh? You have, but it's unlikely that you've realised. It's that thing they do with their lips when they shake their heads, or sometimes if they are particularly tickled they will roll over on their backs and wave their legs in the air. A lip-rippler is the technical term for it. Dob rippled his lips almost loud enough to wake the sleeping humans snoring in their beds in the houses that bordered the country park.

"Ok, so what are you then, a giraffe?"
More ripples followed but Blue wasn't joining in.

"I'm a unicorn. The last unicorn on this island."

This stopped the ripples. Dob knew quite well what a unicorn was. Many of the little girls who came to ride would pretend he was one, as they trotted excitedly along the bridle path securely on his back, usually wearing either a unicorn top, or at the very least a backpack bearing a unicorns image. Invariably the colour pink would be involved. It wasn't great but it was certainly far preferable to being called "My Little Pony." Dob's knowledge of the species was limited but, rainbow mane or not, he knew there was a vital element missing.

"I'm not being rude, I'm really not Blue, but I have to ask. What about the horn?"

Blue smirked with mock indignation. "I don't show what I've got to everyone you know, but I like you soft lad. Hold on to your fetlocks."

She shook her mane, almost in slow motion, like an equine supermodel and the diva that she was. The thick rainbow curtain parted with perfect choreography to reveal a glittering, spectacular horn. It wasn't enormous by any standards, but it was perfectly in proportion. Dob was astonished but certainly not speechless.

"How have you been able to keep that hidden? If you're magic, why are you stuck here in this paddock?!!" He couldn't contain himself, the questions kept coming, but then his voice faltered as he realised. "You're *too* special Blue. You can't stick around looking like this. You're leaving me aren't you?"

It was Blue's turn to ripple her lips. "Have they been feeding you Haribo today? Why don't you just hold your horses and I'll explain everything. Not everyone can see my special qualities, *unless* I wish them to, or *unless* they are really special, like you." Dob suddenly felt rather warm; yes...horses can blush too! "The humans just see I'm a gorgeous white horse, but I *am* a unicorn. Make no mistake." Blue went on to explain her mysterious arrival at the stables all those months ago.

"My clan has lived here for thousands of years, but we were getting fed up of *them*...the people. We travelled all over the place you know, up and down the country, anywhere to find beauty, peace and happiness but they've spoiled it. They make far too much pollution nowadays and there's simply just not enough love or happiness around. That's what we *really* graze on, good vibrations. The grass munching is just for show. Glastonbury being cancelled was the last straw for us; that's our main event when we get fat and happy from the people all having a ball without a care in the world. So it was time for pastures new, but could we decide? No chance. Some said Iceland, because they fancied a cheeky dip in the Blue Lagoon, others favoured Norway...the trolls are supposed to be a boss laugh, but as a group we just couldn't agree and it got a little bit er... heated. I couldn't be doing with it, so I flew off in a huff and I landed here and I've been looking and waiting ever since."

Dob was usually awestruck when Blue spoke to him but just now he felt incredibly sad. He was going to lose the only creature with four legs who had ever been his friend. Blue had not failed to notice this. "Why the long face? I'm not going anywhere without you soft-lad."

Dob really wanted to believe her but how could that be possible? "I can't fly can I? I'm not magic. I'm no good to you Blue, I'm just an ordinary pony."

Her eyes flashed at him with steely blue temper. "Don't you ever think that! You are in no way ordinary! Do you think I would ever have spoken to you if that was the case? Ok, you haven't got a rainbow in your tail but look at you! Those dapples! No wonder those mares over there are so jealous. Do you know

what they'll never have? A heart as kind as yours Dob. That's real magic and I wouldn't be without it. Together, with a little help from my friend Aurora, we can fly *together* wherever we fancy. Now do you believe me scone-head?"

Dob did.

Meteorologists confirmed a rare phenomenon in the skies over Liverpool that night. There had been multiple sightings of the Aurora Borealis, or Northern Lights. It was rare but not unheard of if the conditions were right. What the weather watchers didn't notice were the two equine beauties dancing miles above the earth as the hypnotic green light show traced its way through the night-time sky, taking them far away to their new life together.

The next morning the staff at the riding school were dismayed to find Blue's paddock was empty. The gates were padlocked shut and nothing was visible on their CCTV. She had simply vanished as mysteriously as she'd arrived. They were devastated because, for all her haughty ways, most would admit they'd become rather fond of this curious creature. So fixated were they on what had happened to Blue that no one even noticed Dob was gone as well until the day after. It was obvious that horse thieves were operating in the area. The police were informed, but they never saw Blue and Dob again.

Although Iceland is undoubtedly scenic and the blue lagoon was a tempting prospect, it was simply not tempting enough. Nor could the friendly trolls in Norway persuade our discerning unicorn and her best mate to stop and stay. They wanted to be somewhere decidedly warmer.

If you should ever find yourself on the sunshine island of Ibiza, you may drive past a quiet grassy plain, far, far away from the crazy resorts. If you are very lucky, you might just see two horses grazing happily: one ice white with her mane and tail dyed all the colours of the rainbow, the other a beautiful grey with glitter accentuating the pretty dapples on its back. You will probably smile when you see them. They will probably ripple their lips as you drive away. Fancy doing that to those horses! Only in Ibiza eh?

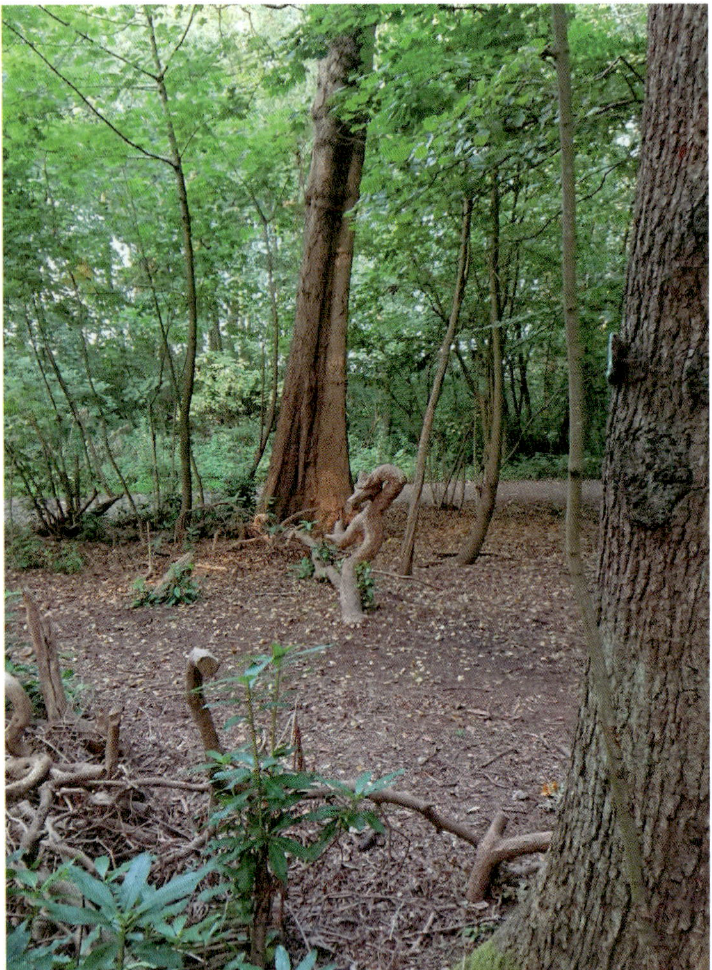

THE DRAGON OF DAM WOOD

She'd never been fitter in her life. Exercise had become her refuge in times of worldwide pandemic. Her body was looking good, possibly better than it had ever done before. The horrible irony was she couldn't do much with it. Cheers COVID 19. No foreign beach holidays for her. No slightly inappropriate bikinis for her age demographic, to show off her frankly killer legs. No man to wonder, as he appreciated how hot she was, how on Earth he'd managed to punch so far above his weight. The best she could do was keep herself busy with bits and bobs and, if she was lucky, lounge in the sunshine in her garden and hope she wasn't being perved at by the neighbours.

She was alone. Full stop. This was depressing and the only thing that she knew to do to drag her out of this spiral of misery was more exercise: walk the bastard off!

In a funny way, lockdown did have its compensations. Her exercise addiction had led to her finally discovering the beauty of her humble neighbourhood.

The giant private housing estate had been her home for fifteen years, but was somewhere she'd never had to take that much notice of until now. Drive off, drive back on, rest, repeat. That had been it before lockdown. However, it turned out that this rabbit warren of humanity was a beautiful mystery waiting to be solved.

As time under lockdown passed and her daily walk (as advised by the government) became routine, she learned all the road names, all the paths and all the shortcuts she had previously ignored. The woman was like a London cabby who had just passed "the knowledge" with flying colours but with no real opportunity to share it.

The paths were her favourite. They were not just short cuts or a convenience; they were a means of escape from the restrictions of the estate, each one leading to proper countryside. Actual fields and woodland were there on her doorstep and she'd had no idea it had even existed before…well, before the world shut down.

She was an early riser, always had been. In times of stress this could be tiresome. You never feel quite so solitary as you do in the early hours. She lived alone so there was no "other" she could roll over and hug for the reassurance she craved. The only thing she could do was get out and walk her worries away.

This was how it started.

One early morning in May, after walking around the estate perimeter road, she was enticed by a pathway she'd never considered taking before. There was a barrier in place, courtesy of the council, designed to prevent those delightful woolly headed youths on their illegal motorbikes from abusing what lay beyond. Feeling unusually confident and curious, she sashayed through the gap and entered what seemed to be another world.

Trees were all around her, providing a dark but welcoming canopy for the pathway ahead. It had been raining that day and the temperature was mild, even at 6.30 am. The scent of warm decaying bark and fermenting leaf mould clothed her swiftly in an embrace of comfort and wellbeing and she immediately felt at least some of her worries melting away. She carried on walking briskly and was amazed at the continuing assault on her senses. Wafting through the clouds of woodland perfume, she had an orchestral accompaniment from what must have been at least a hundred different birds, each serenading her with their song to greet the morning. Her spirits lifted even higher…

Out of the corner of her eye she kept spotting flashes of movement. At first she thought, rather unpleasantly, that it must be rats: you're never supposed to be more than two metres away from one are you? She was wrong. The place was simply alive with grey squirrels, fluffy flinty imps leaping from tree to tree and causing mini tornadoes in the undergrowth. These mischief merchants occasionally ran riot in the nearby suburban, semi-manicured gardens, frustrating those who had green fingers and borderline OCD tendencies. Not today. Their crackpot antics in the half light of that early morning made her smile. It had been a while.

The squirrels weren't her only company. A family of hedgehogs scuttled urgently across her path, like they desperately had somewhere to be, and she was amazed to see an urban fox quietly giving her the eye from a polite distance. This was getting ridiculous now, she felt like a Scouse Snow White; all she needed was the seven dwarves to show up!

While contemplating that decidedly strange train of thought, her eyes were drawn to a wooden sign nailed to an old imperious oak tree: "This way to Narnia." It wasn't actually pointing anywhere definite. There were a few paths she could have picked and she liked the sign all the more for its ambiguity.

I think I'll stick to the main path, she thought, but she reserved the right to be more adventurous at a later date…

Just past the sign, a tune popped into her head out of nowhere, brashly drowning out the morning chorus. The tune in her head was "Vogue" by Madonna, truly a blast from the past. *Where the hell did that come from?*

It was so random that it stopped her in her tracks and that was when she saw it.

Her logical self would have described it as a twisted, gnarled stump of rhododendron with a rather unusual structural quality to it. However, her more imaginative side immediately saw a creature. No, not a creature, more specifically a dragon – and this dragon was frozen, striking a pose, *voguing* just like Madge.

Oh shit I'm losing the plot!

She laughed to herself, took one last look and shook her head before moving on. The song stayed firmly in her head and the very idea of a dragon dancing so stylishly lurked at the back of her mind all day.

The place this woman had discovered that fateful morning was Dam Wood. She knew this because when she reached the end of the main pathway, Liverpool city council had kindly erected a great big sign saying so. She'd lived here all these years and had never even noticed it. How had this place failed to get her attention until now? A bit bemused, but with a definite elevated mood, she returned to the concrete pavement that led her back to reality, certain that today would not be her last visit to that enchanted place.

It became far from it. She could not get the slightly silly notion of the dragon, which was really no more than a rhododendron stump, out of her head. It became a daily pilgrimage for her. She simply had to be there.

Every visit was relished because it was always different. Each change in the weather would herald a fresh dimension to the place for her: a wet spell would wake up legions of fungi, the blustery days would whip the branches of the trees into a wild symphony of glorious chaos. The amount of wildlife she saw increased by the day: rabbits, badgers...

one day she even thought she saw a hare looking at her with wise green eyes. It was wonderful, but there was always one constant: the music that would fill her head

Dah dah dah dah dah Vogue...Vogue...Vogue...Vogue.

Without fail.

It was like an alarm was set off and someone woke up the resident woodland DJ and bingo! It was 1990...in her head anyway. It had stopped being annoying for her. She just wanted to dance.

She always looked at the "dragon" every day. Just in case. She found herself willing to see a change in her demeanour. Yes, the dragon was a "she!" Of course she was and she was always haughty...she was Voguing after all! But the woman wished, just one time, that she could see a change, something to justify her crazy constant notions about what was really just a lump of wood.

This obsession served a strange purpose. It distracted her from the reality of lockdown. She couldn't do much: no work to go to, no shops to go and waste time and money in, no socialising, no man to argue with, no living…not as she remembered it anyway. This dreary existence ceased to matter; she had Madge and the wood. Her daily walks were truly saving her.

The seasons rolled on like seasons do and 2020, the year like no other, dragged humanity along with it like a spoiled child having a tantrum. Daily walks had taken on a new dimension for the woman. It meant *everything* to her. She started to vary the time she went out, edging closer and closer to the darkness, seemingly unafraid of being out alone because in her mind she wasn't alone at all…she had Madge.

It was an oppressively hot evening in August when everything changed.

The stifling humidity had made sleep an impossibility. It was 2am and she was sweating in her bed and it really wasn't pleasant. Unable to stand it a moment longer, she threw on her walking clothes. For some reason she also put her sequinned, rainbow bum bag on. She had worn it at Festivals, when they still had festivals. She had an overwhelming need to sparkle, just a little.

The journey from her front door to the entrance of Dam Wood barely registered; she was a woman on a mission, drawn inexplicably to the leafy wonderland like her life depended on it.

Tonight was different, she felt it with all her senses and something more...was it her heart? She didn't know, but she was dizzy with unexplained excitement. The aroma of the woodland was heavy and more intoxicating to her than ever before. Every sound she heard seemed fine tuned, as sharp as a pinprick. Each twig that snapped underneath her trainers was like a tiny whip crack. Maybe a thunderstorm was coming. It was almost as if she could feel the electricity all around her.

It should have been pitch black in those woods. The leafy canopy was still full and verdant, providing an impenetrable shield from the starlight and the streetlights. Except that night it wasn't. There was a glow, a very definite glow in the middle distance in the woods up ahead.

She should have been scared.

Thoughts were racing through her head. *Who could it be? Were those rumours about it being a bit of a dogging paradise actually true?*

She hoped not, but right now she didn't care if it was. Curiosity got the better of her and on she walked without the least hesitation.

The glow was joined very soon by a constant thud thud thudding sound. Music was playing. Maybe it was a rave. So what if it was? She carried on.

It soon became apparent that the glow was getting brighter and the driving beat stronger the nearer she got to the Narnia sign. Her heart began to beat a fraction faster in her chest. At first she couldn't see anything specific, just an ever intensifying glow. The woodland seemingly had its own self-generating light force.

It was then that the fallen sapling she had walked past a thousand times rose up from the woodland floor all by itself and parted like a heavy velvet curtain on a theatre stage. It was opening night and time to leave her version of reality behind!

The rising sapling had revealed a fox, wearing a very slick black dinner suit, acting as a bouncer on a beautiful quilted black leather door. He looked her up and down for quite some time before smiling and nodding at her to enter, which of course she did.

She was instantly surrounded by all those woodland animals she had encountered on her numerous daily walks over the past few months. They were looking at her like *she* was some sort of exhibit. You would think being stared at by a crew of hyperactive squirrels and a gang of half cut hedgehogs was strange enough but, she quickly realised, they were in a *nightclub* and it was banging!

Holding court in the middle of the dance floor was Madge. Our dragon was real. She was a beauty with fiery red eyes wearing, with effortless style, an impossibly sexy black trouser suit, just like Madonna wore in the video she made for "Vogue!" She tilted her fabulous noble head just a fraction and stared dramatically in the direction the sequinned new arrival. There was a hint of a smile in those eyes of hers and her voice was as seductive and smooth as the smoke that spiralled out of her nostrils.

"Strike a pose…I've been waiting for you," the dragon purred.

The woman knew that, however crazy this seemed, she'd been waiting for this moment all her life. She danced.

In the misty light of dawn, the oddly shaped rhododendron stump was there like it had been every day. Joggers jogged past it, dogs cocked their legs on it and rain rained on it. Nothing different, nothing to see. People walked past it without even noticing it was there. They didn't even notice the sequinned bum bag looped over an adjacent stump, almost as if it had been left behind because it wasn't needed anymore.

Sometimes people only see the things that they are *meant* to see.

Somewhere…she was still dancing.

POETRY

THANK YOU

THANK YOU

Through the conservatory window lies my
whole world of ten weeks or more
My modest garden of tiny proportions
I've taken you for granted for decades
Little knowing you would one day rescue
me in so many ways
Hidden corners barely tended
Starved of my attention
Now I smother you like a needy friend
You hold no grudge
Instead returning my love one hundred fold
Every day a new surprise
A flower I've not planted unselfishly appears
A gift from nature most welcome in my darkest hours
I've played my part in adding to my Eden
Watching the plants I've carefully
placed like a mother hen
Waging a war against the evil squirrel determined
to ruin my paradise
A beautiful distraction
My safe space
Our space
The place I want to stay
What's so good about beyond this?
I miss it less, the closer I come to reacquainting
myself with reality.

THE ILLUSTRATED MAN

THE ILLUSTRATED MAN

I know it's rude to stare but I can't help it.
I'm like a magpie, attracted to the colours.
Each picture has me guessing at the meaning.
Are they connected, or as random as the weather?
I'd love to ask, but shyness will prevent me.
Maybe it's better to wonder and imagine.
Then my eyes stumble on the image on his hand.
A couple kissing, with passion to be envied.
Two simple words alongside tell the story.
Their kiss is love. A love that's never ending.

WHAT IF?

WHAT IF?

What if I'd never known you?
What if we'd never met?
How different would my life be?
I never could forget
That we are like one person
So matched in every way
Each part of you is part of me
The reason for my day
I might have had a good life
A different one for sure
But life without you can't replace
our love forevermore

ABOUT THE AUTHOR

Paula Page

A quietly spoken scouser (yes, they do exist!) and a creative late bloomer who enjoys surprising herself and others with what she can do when she tries.

Printed in Great Britain
by Amazon